THE VERY HUNGRY CATERPILLAR

by Eric Carle

SCHOLASTIC INC.

New York Toronto London Auckland Sydney

ALSO BY ERIC CARLE

1,2,3, to the Zoo
The Very Hungry Caterpillar (miniature edition)
The Very Busy Spider
The Honeybee and the Robber
Chip Has Many Brothers (written by Hans Bauman)
Do You Want to Be My Friend? (miniature edition)
Have You Seen My Cat? (miniature edition)
The Very Busy Spider (miniature edition)
Animals Animals
The Very Quiet Cricket

ISBN 0-590-03029-9
ISBN 0-590-29275-7 (meets NASTA specifications)
Copyright © 1969, 1987 by Eric Carle.
All rights reserved.
Published by Scholastic Inc., 555 Broadway, New York, NY 10012,
by arrangement with Penguin Putnam Inc.
SCHOLASTIC and associated logos are trademarks and/or
registered trademarks of Scholastic Inc.

45 44 43 42 41 40 39 38 37 36   08   11 10 09 08

Printed in Malaysia

For my sister Christa

In the light
of the moon
a little egg
lay on a leaf.

One Sunday morning the warm sun came up and—pop!—out of the egg came a tiny and very hungry caterpillar.

He started to look for some food.

On Saturday
he ate through
one piece of
chocolate cake, one ice-cream cone, one pickle, one slice of Swiss cheese, one slice of salami,

On Friday
he ate through
five oranges,
but he was still
hungry.

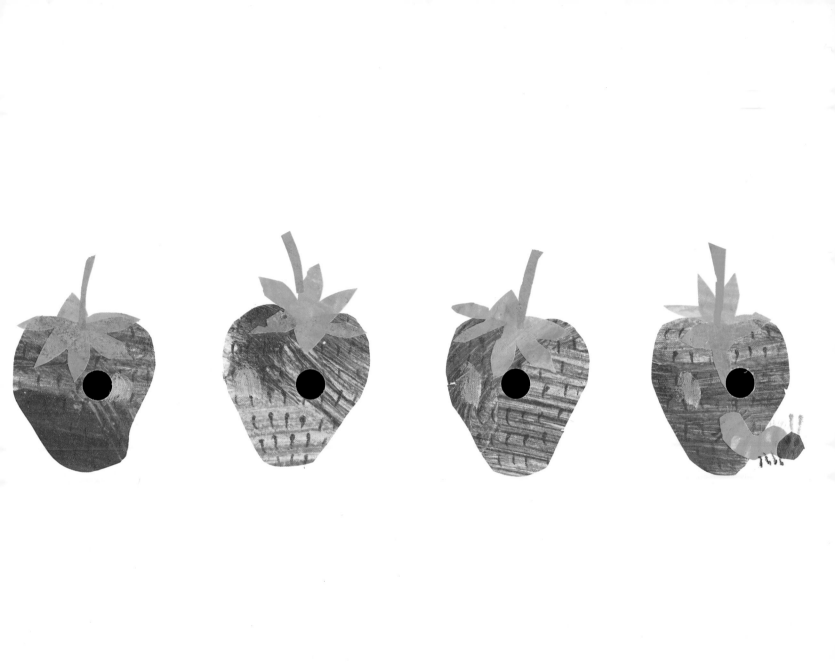

On Thursday
he ate through
four strawberries,
but he was still
hungry.

On Friday
he ate through
five oranges,
but he was still
hungry.

On Saturday
he ate through
one piece of
chocolate cake, one ice-cream cone, one pickle, one slice of Swiss cheese, one slice of salami,

The next day was Sunday again.
The caterpillar ate through
one nice green leaf,
and after that he felt
much better.

Now he wasn't hungry any more—and he wasn't a little caterpillar any more.
He was a big, fat caterpillar.

He built a small house, called a cocoon, around himself. He stayed inside for more than two weeks. Then he nibbled a hole in the cocoon, pushed his way out and . . .

he was a beautiful butterfly!

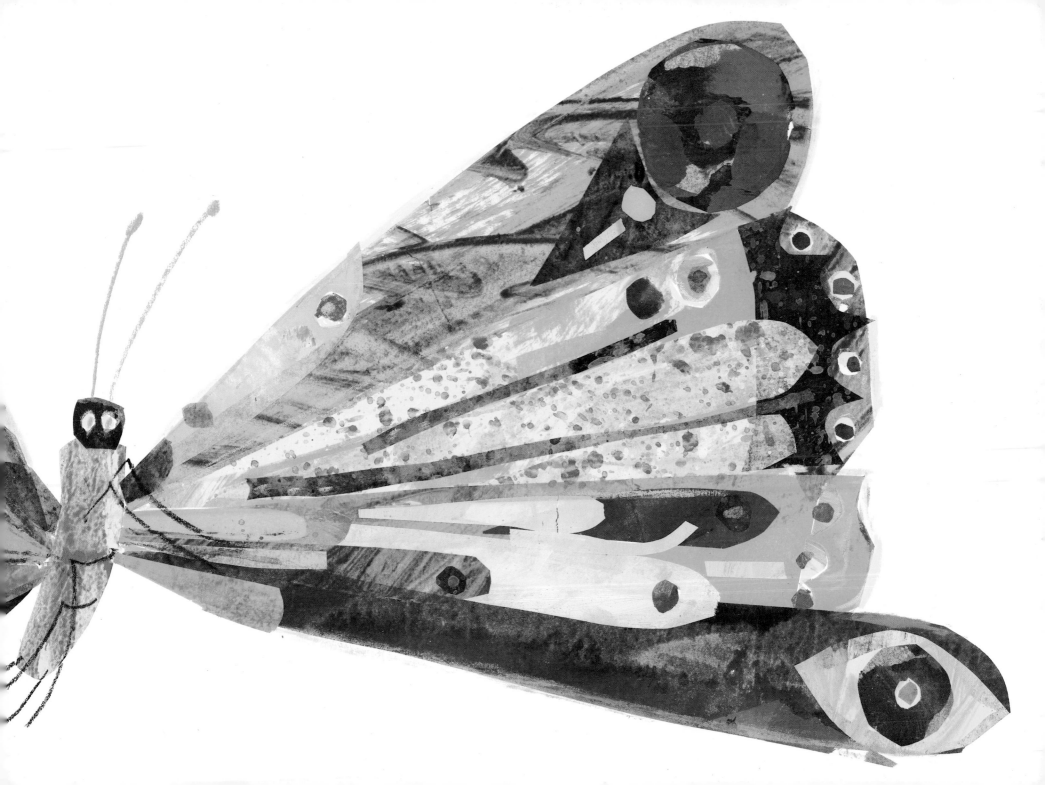

On Wednesday
he ate through
three plums,
but he was still
hungry.

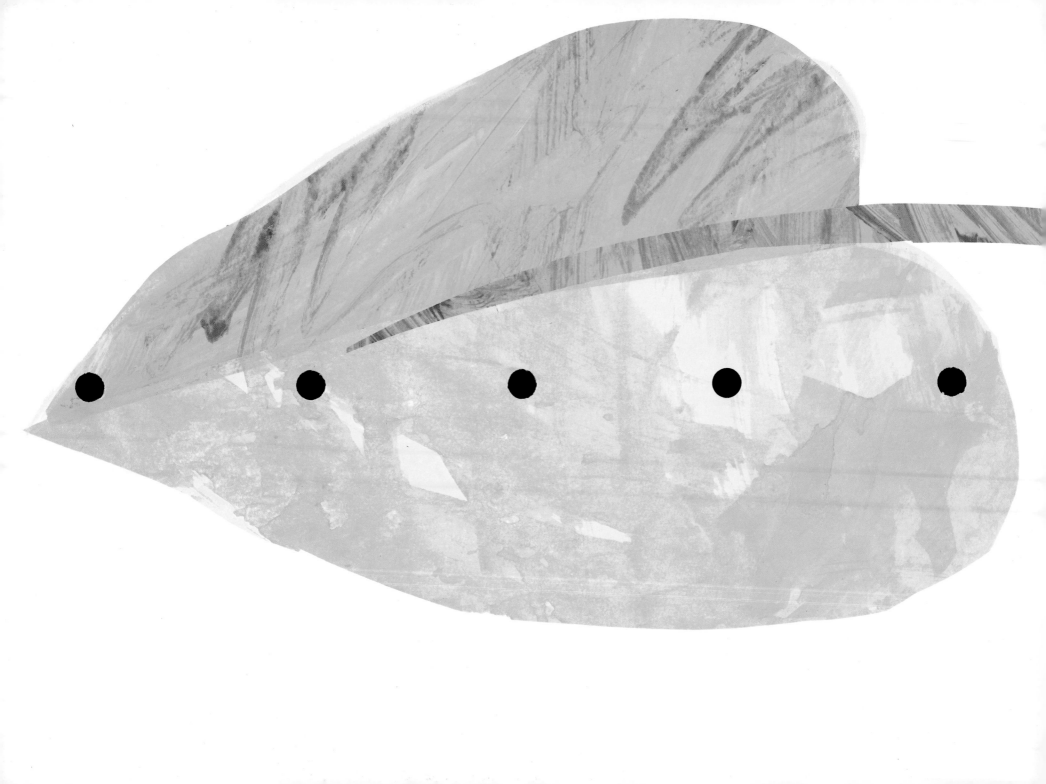

one lollipop, one piece of cherry pie, one sausage, one cupcake, and one slice of watermelon.

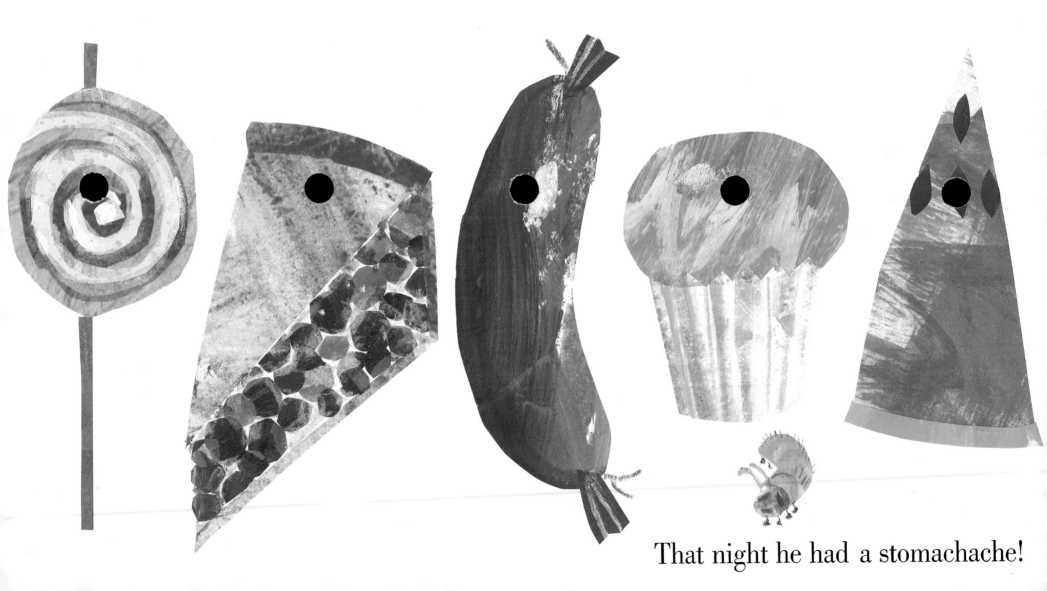

That night he had a stomachache!